Handle With Care

Clever Fox
PUBLISHING

Chennai • Bangalore

Handle With Care

LITTLE THINGS MATTER

26 Short Stories for Parents from a Teacher's Perspective

Ramaa Shankar

ISBN 13: 978-93-90025-90-9
ISBN 10: 93-90025-90-7

Published by CLEVER FOX PUBLISHING

Dedicated to my mother, Srimati Saroja Krishnamurthi for her support and motivation and to my father, Late Shri D. Krishnamurthi, who was and is my inspiration.

About the Author

 **Ramaa Shankar** is a senior post graduate teacher in a school in Delhi where she has more than 26 years of work and life experience. Teaching is her passion of choice. Accountancy, business studies, classical dance and creative choreography are the four fronts of her prescriptive pedagogy.

Ramaa received her senior school certificate from DTEA Mandir Marg in New Delhi and completed her Bachelor's and Master's degree programmes in Commerce, with Honours, both from the prestigious Shri Ram College of Commerce, University of Delhi. She also holds a Bachelor's degree in Education, a Master's in Business Administration and cleared the National Eligibility Test (NET). Her academic credentials and pedagogic experience are bolstered and supplemented by her forays and achievements in classical dance.

A top-grade artiste of Doordarshan Kendra, India, she is known for her proficiency in the classical dance forms of Kuchipudi and Bharatanatyam. She has given several performances in India and abroad and featured on multiple occasions in the National Program of Dance on the Doordarshan National Network–a weekly national broadcast with the country's finest performing artistes. She is a recipient of the National Cultural Talent Scholarship and Merit Scholarship, awarded by the Government of India. She was conferred the title of **Natya Tilakam** by Ganesh Natyalaya, New Delhi and **Singar Mani** by Sur Singar Samsad, Mumbai.

She focuses on making classical dance relevant for the present generation and attempts to weave it with learning for effectiveness. Her most recent forays have been to stress upon water conservation through a Kuchipudi dance recital on Doordarshan, teaching Henri Fayol's principles of management through choreography recognised by CBSE and the presentation of dance ballets on themes of Gandhian principles, national integration and global harmony.

Contents

Preface

PARENTS AND TEACHERS love to give sermons to children. We correct them for their bad behaviour, for being disrespectful and for disobeying instructions. Empirical evidence from child psychology and anecdotal experience from our lived experiences teach us to pause those sermons and seek alternate measures. Behaviour that is considered "abnormal" on the part of children is, almost always, a cry for help.

This book is an attempt to condense twenty-six years of my interactions into stories of information and insight. The English language offers twenty-six building blocks, that is, alphabets, to communicate complex emotions into simple stories. I have attempted to find different themes, issues and ideas from my experiences and present them impactfully.

The aim of these short stories is not prescription. Each child is unique in their own way, just like every combination of the alphabet as a word, sentence or essay conveys different meaning. My objective is to convey to both parents and teachers that children are not robots. I would like society to think of children uniquely instead of treating them as cold statistics.

Each child is special. They are a bundle of aspirations and possibilities. Most teachers will agree that we are able to act only with limited knowledge about students. We see the tip of the iceberg, much of which remains unseen making behavioral patterns extremely difficult to unravel.

My experience has taught me that the most important element in the learning process is communication. When children are small, they are extremely frank, but as they grow, they don't necessarily share everything with their parents. The difficult part with teenagers is to be able to understand what is not being said. A flicker in the eyes, shaking of a head and a subtle turn in a different direction may be indicating something we should pay attention to.

If children are a complicated mystery to teachers, they are a complex puzzle to parents. While genes and memes combine in interesting ways to construct our humanity, the struggle and contributions between nature and nurture remains an unsolved problem. The cause-effect relationship between good parenting and balanced children is yet to be decoded. There is no one right answer. There can't be standardization.

India, half a century ago, had far more relaxed parenting. Globalization, interconnectedness and population explosion, amidst increasing urbanization and technology expansion, has created tired, stressed out, obsessive and perfection-seeking parents.

This book, written amidst the world's first global pandemic in a century, has helped me understand the unnecessary rat race amongst parents who bring up unhappy children. Instead of being overbearing, justifying strictness, emphasizing sacrifice and stridently seeking outcome-oriented glory, I feel the world and its children would be a happier place with less judgmental, calmer and more accepting parents.

At the end of the day, parents and teachers are collaborators and each must try to understand the other's point of view. Demanding parents transfer their stress to teachers in many cases, whilst teachers make judgment without fully knowing the personal history of a child or parent. Often, teachers find it difficult when there is unhealthy competition between students, which emanates frequently, from parents or their choices. Sometimes, parents walk out of joint families or marriage as an institution. They justify several actions in the name of the child without necessarily anticipating its effect on them or evaluating the true nature of those actions.

Children will find it difficult to be happy if their parents aren't happy. Even the environment that is provided to the baby in the womb affects the child. The sound of laughter, jingle of temple bells, happy chatter around a warm and fragrant kitchen and evocative fresh coffee frothily poured from a height provide positive vibrations. The bickering of relatives, fighting amongst parents, broken pipes and vessels, sickness of mind and body and tense finances can accelerate negativity in a family.

There is a clear ability of perception of good and bad vibrations that a child feels from the parents. For example, I used to recite the prayer "Vishnu Sahasranamam" twice a day when my child was in the womb. I was pleasantly surprised to hear him recite the same happily when he was just three years old. Neither of us are dogmatically religious but that feeling of positivity somehow got communicated through the frequencies of loving non-verbal communication.

A peaceful atmosphere does a lot of good to the foetus in the womb. Once the child is born, the family atmosphere makes all the difference. The emotional development of a child helps him in the various roles he has to play in his adult life including parenting. The prevalence of depression, anxiety and mental illness is real, but using these words to trigger action must be carefully done, because sometimes they are used loosely and not fully understood. It is also imperative that the school curriculum has a basic course in mental health which helps them take on life's challenges.

Certain items on the Indian news airwaves further triggered me into writing this book:

- A student, who gets admission into IIT, through affirmative action, goes into depression as he is unable to cope up with the curriculum and the environment.
- After ten years of graduating from an MBA program at a renowned business school, a young man kills his wife because he is unable to manage work stress.
- A student in twelfth grade commits suicide after doing poorly in a physics exam for the fear of disappointing her father.
- A forty year old man brutally rapes a school-going student.

The environment in which our children are being brought up is excruciating to say the least. Injustice on the grounds of class, caste, language, gender, region, religion, identity, ideas and physical constructs are very common. Even with great teachers, loving parents and happy environments, there can be no guarantee for success and happiness. In my experience, our attitude and respect towards girls and women along with a revival of the role of extended families can help ameliorate this suffering.

Inculcate respect towards women and girls

There has been a tendency to forget the malaise and ills of society continuously even as law and order worsens especially with respect to crimes against women and girls. As a society, we have asked our girl children to ignore voyeurs, stalkers, sexual harassers and even rapists and murderers. The poor condition of rule of law and social progress has taken away individual freedoms and collective liberties of half our population.

Girls are advised to ignore such miscreants while travelling in public transport. They are asked not to go out after a certain time or to a particular venue for their own safety. A girl is supposed to be protected by her father, brother, husband and children throughout her life. Today, it has become unsafe to step out of the colony. Tomorrow, it may become unsafe inside the colony. She has lost independence and freedom.

We can't keep correcting the girls and promote a lawless society. We have to ensure implementation of law and order and that begins by saying no when any wrong act occurs. A lawless society snatches the charm and glee from a girl's life, interferes with seemingly harmless and obvious decisions of education and employment due to fear and most importantly scars another generation of future families into status quo.

We have to ensure that girls are protected as independent and creative members of society. They should be taught to be alert, made strong and brave physically and mentally and most importantly be supported through action rather than words. The true potential of an individual can never come out if the person is fearful. Sometimes, it can lead to mental sickness. We must save our girl children and empower them to save our society.

Reviving grand old collective wisdom

India has always placed greater importance and practical relevance to an extended family. Grandparents, blood relatives, familial relations and other near and dear ones, form the first friendships and relationships for a child. Their interactions shape the child's development.

It is important that grandparents are just and fair. They should not differentiate between their grandchildren. Do's and don'ts cannot indiscriminately apply to one and not to the other. In some joint families, as they are called in India, children of the son who is living abroad are treated specially. His wife, who never helps, is treated royally. The other son, who is with his parents, running a middle-class household, coping with all his duties, is questioned. His children are disciplined and expected to adjust much more.

Similarly, a joint family or an extended family must not support a child when actions are incorrect as that results in wrong inferences by the child. Powerplay and politics in families may lead to further emotional imbalance amongst children. It takes a village to raise a child. It is important that the village furthers values such as kindness, dignity, individualism, collectivism, rationalism, freedom, liberty and prosperity.

As a member of the teaching community, I request the parents and society to understand the behavior of children in the right perspective. I have varied experiences with children in academics and dance, and have an innate interest in children and why they do what they do. My advice to everyone is not to be judgmental. As most of us are interested in providing a good environment for children who are the future of the world, we must not indulge in competitive parenting and mechanistic education.

The stories in this book are an attempt to frame context and stimulate conversations that lead us to become more conscious and better parents and teachers. These short stories are based on several real-life experiences. However, before we get to the stories, I must declare my inspirations, for my fiction learnt immensely from my reality.

First and foremost, I thank my students over twenty-six years of teaching in various subjects and classes for enriching my life with their stories, trials, tribulations, victories and joys. My son, Roshan, is the reason for my enthusiasm and perpetual learning in life. As a mother, I know that I have to keep evolving, very similar to the role of a teacher. This book would not have been possible without the support of my husband, Shankar. I dedicate this book to my parents and teachers from my school and college for their support and encouragement and allowing me to find and walk a path that was my own.

Here are twenty-six cases and stories, picked from the alphabets of life, hoping to provide you an A-Z understanding of children.

Allergic Asha

ASHA WAS AN asthmatic child. When she was in eleventh grade, you could mistake her for being in seventh grade due to her small build. She lived in a joint family and hardly interacted with her mother as she was the eldest with many younger siblings. Her grandmother took care of her. Asha's grandmother was ambitious. She was a retired school Principal and very demanding. She could not accept the fact that Asha did not have the aptitude to do mathematics or accountancy.

Asha sought love from her mother. Her mother was not educated and her hands were full. Asha's asthma was usually triggered during the change of season. She was also allergic to examinations and dreaded parent teacher meetings which were mostly attended by her grandmother.

One day, all the students were to go to the playground for sports day practice. Though Asha was not practising, she did not want to stay alone. So, she moved to the playground with her class and class teacher. Suddenly, she became breathless. Her class teacher ran to get an inhaler from one of her asthmatic friends who was a teacher in the same grade. She had an inhaler in her handbag which she promptly gave. Asha was rushed to school premises after providing first aid and a call to her family was made. Fortunately, her father came immediately and took her to the hospital. This could have been disastrous. The class teacher later explained to the father about unhealthy comparisons and its negative effect on Asha. She requested him to keep her happy and appreciate her other skills. This made a big difference.

Her father, Ajeet, recalled his childhood days vividly. It was a blast from the past. He recalled how his mother discriminated against him because he was not good in science and pampered his brother who was a bright child. He did well later in his life and his brother, who went abroad, hardly kept in touch. Ajeet wondered about the use of money that his brother made when he couldn't be humane and of service to his family. His mother was also unhappy about it although she never mentioned it. Ajeet vowed to talk to his mother with this example and to accept Asha as she was.

Asha had a pleasant personality and good inter personal skills. She was very good with nail art and henna designs. She also loved to dance. After schooling, she did a course in travel and tourism management which she enjoyed. She made a lot of friends and later took up a job as a travel consultant. She met her life partner there and got married after a year of courtship. They moved from India to Detroit in the United States where she now lives a happy life. Her asthma problem is now well under control.

It is important to understand and accept the world and its children as it is, instead of seeing the world that we want. Only then can we be the change we want to see.

Bold and Beautiful

GOWRI WAS THE first born of her parents. She was beautiful and was excellent in academics. Immediately after she completed her graduation, it was decided to marry her off to her father's friend's son, Anant, keeping business growth and continuity in mind. Gowri was disappointed as she wanted to pursue an MBA and be independent. Anant, on the other hand, was a typical pampered child of a traditional and rather patriarchal family. He was an introvert who despised going out or socializing, contrary to the extroverted and happy Gowri who thrived in fun and new environments.

It was a grand Indian wedding. However, she was not happy with the marriage from day one. The Gymkhana Club which Gowri frequented for sports and leisure was suddenly out of bounds. She decided that she would ensure that the marriage does not work and would find an exit. Being a legally informed and clever girl, she collected grounds for divorce methodically and gave no choice to Anant but to agree for the same.

She decided not to go to her parents' house. She was an independent woman and would live life on her own terms. She did her MBA and took up a job in a multi-national corporation which also provided her furnished accommodation. She had proved her point. But now, life was getting to be boring. She started depending on alcohol to some extent.

It was at the club that she met Rao, a young and successful industrialist. The best part was that it was not his father's business. It was his own start-up that succeeded because of his intelligence and initiative. He was also a sportsperson, very outgoing and charming. He was tall, handsome and had a great sense of humour. His attitude towards Gowri's professional career was positive and empowering. In due course, they became close, got married and had a son, Karthik. Once Karthik was of school going age, they put him in the best school in the town.

Gowri had no patience and Rao had no time to give to the child. Both Gowri and Rao were ambitious and had become workaholics. Success had become an addiction. They felt let down because they expected their son to be bright and not slow and sloppy. Often, it would irritate them when they heard him singing a song and lost in his own world of music while doing his homework.

Primary school itself saw Karthik becoming demanding and sometimes aggressive in his classes and amongst his peers. He was looked after mostly by the cook, maid and the driver. He got no positive affirmation from his parents or their time. The class teacher wrote a couple of messages to the parents requiring their presence for a meeting. Gowri paid no attention to it. Finally, a call came from the school Principal and the parents were forced to visit school.

The Principal tried to convey his opinion about the child and saw the need for co-operation amongst the argumentative parents. However, the Principal didn't succeed. When they walked out of the office, the Principal could hear Rao shouting at Gowri for not nurturing the kid properly. Gowri too screamed at Rao saying that it was a joint responsibility. Both parents started discussing boarding school as soon as they got into the car as the only fail-safe to discipline their son. They figured that it was the lack of strictness that was missing with Karthik and not taking this step would turn him from bad to worse. Karthik asked himself if he was so bad that his parents wanted to get rid of him. He felt that he was a burden to his parents.

As planned, his parents put him in a boarding school. At the school, Kartik got a lot of love from his music teacher who found a potential musician in him. Kartik did not miss his parents and was not keen to go back home during the vacations. He had found his inspiration in D'Silva ma'am, who had brought out his love for classical music.

After school, when the world rushed for deified universities, corporate jobs and glitzy startups, he took up music as his vocation and profession. He could never find a way to connect deeply and meaningfully with his parents whom he thought had offloaded him as an outsourced job-work for completion to a boarding school. His music and magical voice, whilst popular and award-winning, had a sense of sadness that was still trying to speak to his parents. He got love from everyone but always felt that something important was missing. He instituted a school where young talent was promoted and taken care of comprehensively to ensure that no talent suffered from having unfulfilled potential.

Sometimes bad decisions don't have terrible outcomes. However, they do cause heartburn, pain and avoidable suffering for the parents and the child. Parenting is a huge responsibility and like any other critical human process requires commitment.

People are not born with parenting skills but need to cultivate it. Children who love their parents unconditionally should not be blamed but rather an attempt to understand their psyche and emotional state is important.

Caring Chetna

Hema, an Economics teacher, felt helpless. Her student Chetna was irregular, tardy and never completed her assignments on time. Whenever the teacher wrote a note to her parents, there was no response. Hema was afraid that Chetna would not be able to pass the senior secondary school board exams. Hema took stock of the situation and decided to have a conversation.

Chetna was from Jharkhand and was from a poor family. Her parents had migrated to Delhi in search of work. They were successful in getting employment. It was then that her sister, a child with special needs, was born. Her father could not take the stress of handling the child. Gradually, he took to drinking. He became an alcoholic in due course and started beating up his wife if she did not give him money at night for alcohol. Chetna could hardly sleep at night. Her mother had to rush for work in the morning as she was the sole breadwinner. Her father later deserted them. Chetna had to complete the household chores and ensure that her younger sister, Karishma, was bathed and fed. Due to this, she could not attend school regularly or on time.

The picture of Chetna in Hema's mind was completely different before this conversation. Very often, we do not understand the context of the child, the family environment and the effort taken by such children to reach school! Hema appreciated Chetna's courteous behavior in spite of withstanding so must stress at a young age.

She resolved to help out Chetna as she could not afford tuitions. After school, the teacher would share her lunch with Chetna and help her with the subject. She would talk to her at length about her younger sister and work at home. Hema picked themes from Chetna's life for her writing assignments. This helped Chetna find an outlet for her feelings and also contextualized economics from happenings in her daily life.

She also took the opportunity to counsel Chetna to focus on her studies so that she can take up work and be a source of strength to her mother. The teacher would also drop her home, before going to her residence, reinforcing her support to her personally and academically. In the car, they would have a conversation about Karishma and Chetna's eyes would light up as she narrated what all her little sister did. Somehow, all the school work and household responsibilities became an exciting activity to look forward to, instead of a burdensome chore.

Chetna passed the class twelve board exams with flying colours and got to pursue a degree in clinical psychology and now works with children with various special needs in a private school in Delhi. Hema found that her true success came not just in the board exam results but also in making a student's future.

The importance of communication should be recognized by the teacher. Communication should be two-way, in fact

more from the child to the teacher. Teachers should not be judgmental, must have patience to listen, wisdom to understand and speak carefully. The choice of words can have a deep impact on the child. As a gardener would say, when a flower does not bloom, you fix the environment and not the flower.

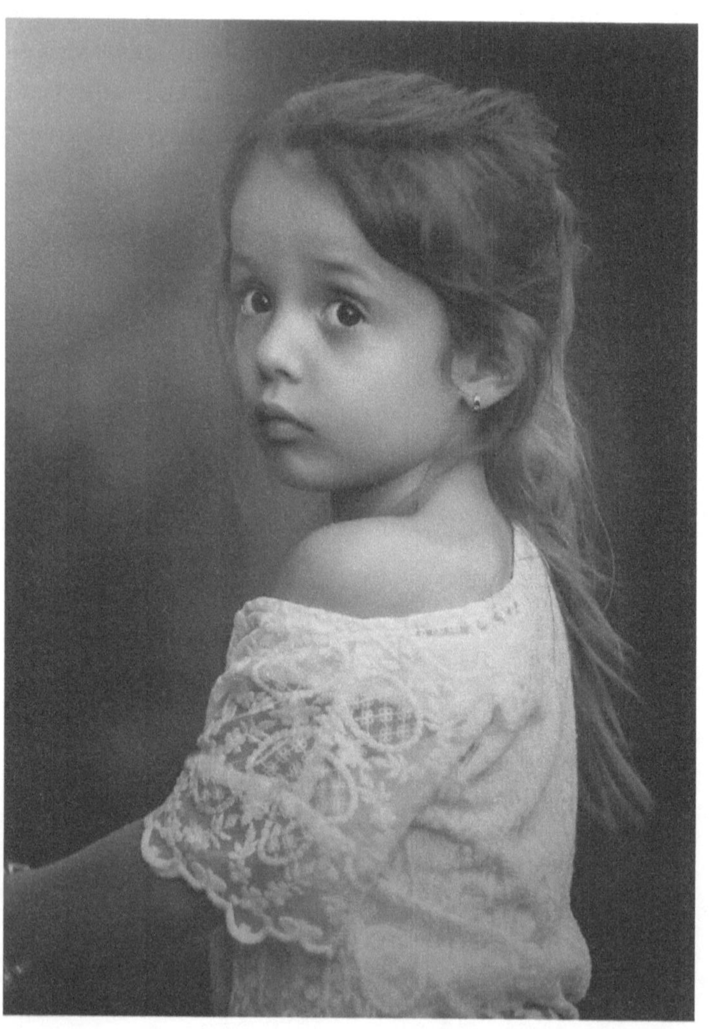

Daddy Dearest

RAJINI, A SEVEN-YEAR old, was a carefree child. She preferred to wear shorts and t-shirts rather than frocks and dresses. She was cheerful and good in academics. She took part in all extra-curricular activities. She had two younger siblings, a brother and a sister. Her mother was a housewife. Her father took keen interest in her activities and co-operated with the class teacher.

It was clear that her dad was her hero. She admired him immensely. She liked to eat dinner with him when he cooked her favourite meal, rice and chicken curry. He would also wash all the dishes and keep them spotless clean as her mother did not like non-vegetarian food. He would play cricket with her on holidays and treat her equal to a son, which was rare. She enjoyed climbing trees, jumping from heights and trekking which her mother would forbid. Her mother would admonish her and tell her to behave like a girl.

On Children's Day, as her father was leaving office, he called up as usual to find out what his dear daughter wanted. Every year this was a ritual. This time she demanded a foot-ball and her father promised to buy it before coming home. Rajini was eagerly waiting for her father. It usually took him an hour to reach home but he did not. Rajini was restless and her family tried to call him but without a response. Time was ticking away. It was past mid night when she learnt that her father was involved in a fatal road accident. It was as if the little world of this family had crumbled down. They couldn't even comprehend what had happened. It took a few days for the tragedy to sink in. When the police gave the belongings from the accident site, a football was there. Rajini was overwhelmed and could not control tears flowing down her eyes.

When Rajini's mother approached her in-laws for assistance, they blamed her for the accident and wanted to do nothing with the family. When she spoke to her brother, he seemed a little aloof as he had his own problems.

When the breadwinner of the family dies, it is extremely difficult for the family. All the so-called close relatives were just hoping that these people would not add to their burden. They kept a distance and didn't offer a helping hand. Her mother had the tough task of bringing up three children.

The decades ahead were arduous and stressful but the family got through them. Rajini grew up, she did well in studies and was employed overseas in a multi-national company. Looking at her mother's plight, Rajini wanted to be financially independent and was not interested in marriage. She also grew bitter at family as an institution when she reminded herself of the times when those of her parents were unavailable and unreachable. Rajini was her father's little girl and his accident killed her in more ways than one.

Sometimes, despite our best efforts and intentions, difficult times approach us through the stroke of fate and the

improbability of bad occurrences. A support structure from an extended family can be helpful to ameliorate pain and suffering. It can be hard at times to catch up with our relatives in this modern age of nuclear families but it is useful to keep an ear out for a silent scream for help armed with a helping hand.

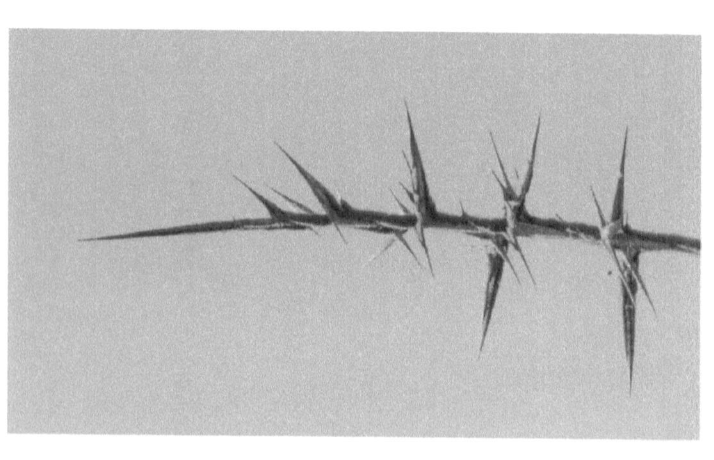

Eyewitness

ANAND WAS UNSURE of what was happening. He had lost his mother when he was just a few months old but somehow felt a lot of love for her. He was brought up by his grandmother as his father had to work as a salesman at a wine shop for long hours. Ten-year old Anand hardly met his father. He had to leave for school early when his father would be asleep and as his father came late from work, Anand would be asleep.

The most important person in his life was his elder sister Khushi, who was in class two when their mother died. She was an extrovert and got along with everyone. She would comfort her grandmother, play with her brother, and wait for her father to return home to have dinner with him. Their father, Girish, did not remarry. His mother was getting frail and old and had to be sent back to her hometown. During this period, his neighbor, Sherry, would pack and give him lunch. He started developing a fondness for her. Girish, who was an introvert, started exchanging notes about the household with her. He realized Sherry aunty, as the children called her, had become close to Khushi as well. Sherry aunty would make breakfast and lunch in the morning for all three of them; in the evening she would return from work and cook their dinner. She would wait for Girish to arrive and then give him dinner.

However, conversations between father and son came to a halt amidst presumptions and misunderstandings. Khushi could understand her father's feelings and Sherry aunty's needs. Sherry aunty filled in the vacuum which even their own aunt could not. She also started attending the Parent Teacher meeting of Khushi and Anand.

Anand was upset. He stopped communicating. His academic performance touched an all-time low. Somehow, he managed to pass the senior secondary board examinations and took up a job at a call center. When Khushi got married, he moved out of the house.

When we look at it from different perspectives, everyone seems trapped. Sherry was in an arranged marriage to a man who she did not find attractive. She bore him two children fulfilling her societal duties. Going to Girish's house was exciting for her. Her insensitive husband would be sleeping anyway. She would go early in the morning to Girish's place, cook for them and return home after spending some quality time with Girish. He would help her in every way without her having to ask him. It was like telepathy with an unparalleled emotional connect. If she wanted something, he knew. It was such a happy time in Girish' s house. He was also generous with gifts unlike her miserly husband. The shrouded relationship was perhaps because of societal pressures. No one could speak their mind.

At the same time, no one would ever be able to understand what Anand witnessed and felt. He longed for his real mother and couldn't accept someone else in her place.

On his part, Anand's father felt that he had sacrificed everything for his children and that he did not remarry although he was only thirty-five when his wife passed away. With two kids and a job, he had his hands full. Though initially, he took help from his mother, the winters in Delhi became difficult for her. When the friendly neighbour, Sherry, offered to take care, he felt it was a blessing in disguise. Their kids were going to the same school and the arrangement seemed godsend. Little did he understand that Anand would feel differently. Anand, a quiet child, had kept his feelings locked up and never raised his voice against his father. Though he had been fuming all along at his father's priorities, when he got older, he decided to move out as soon as he became financially independent. He wanted a breath of fresh air. He was simply tolerating whatever was happening, though he really did not understand fully.

Sensitive children find it difficult to be understood and don't find it easy to communicate. Did any of Anand's teachers have any idea about his innermost thoughts? Was there a possibility to resolve this familial fracture without the eventual amputation? Did his family understand his resentment? Did his friends really know what he was going through? Our lives are the sum of many pasts and it is important for teachers, students and parents to connect the dots backwards at times.

Follow Your Dreams

SHARAD REFUSED TO let go of his mother while he was being dropped in school. It was his first day in nursery. The guard forcibly took the child to his class. Sharad was in tears. His class teacher, Shubha, started distracting him by giving him some toys. The toddler did not stop wailing. Shubha gave him a set of crayons and drawing paper and Sharad calmed down. He had drawn bright blue flowers in various forms. He had coloured the leaves red. The teacher gave him a hug. She felt that there was a creative artist within him.

As he grew, Sharad won prizes in many painting competitions held in school. In middle school, he also won some inter-school competitions. In high school, his academic performance became a cause for concern. He could not devote as much time in studies. His parents and teachers thought that the passion for painting was a distraction and felt that it should stop. Seeing the conflict at hand, he was given lessons on time management by his teacher, which helped him a lot in managing art and academics. It was at this time, when he was in class twelve, that he won a national level painting competition. Sharad decided to take it as his profession. He knew that art was an expression of himself.

After school, he took up courses in animation in which he excelled. He took up a job and became financially independent. He grew professionally, continued his learning and took up art direction. Today, he is one of the leading art directors. He recalls his art teacher telling him to follow the shape while colouring and think about nothing else. His advice to youngsters is "Follow your dreams".

The road not taken is hard and perilous. Love, dedication and interest shown by parents and teachers towards a child's desire and passion can move mountains.

Guilty?

Sunita was the only child in the Thakur family in Mumbai. She was everyone's favorite not only at home but also in school. She was helpful, generous and loving. She was excellent in academics. She would not fall sick even for a day. She was punctual and had perfect attendance. When she was in class eight, the school organized a picnic to Goa. Sunita joined the group eagerly. On reaching Goa, all of them freshened up and went for a stroll in the beach.

As they walked along the shore, they were all excited to see the water and the waves. Sunita and her friends started going closer into the water. All her friends knew swimming. All of a sudden, one of her friends pushed her into the water. Sunita got frightened and screamed. On hearing her screams, her best friend rescued her. She also reprimanded the girl who had pushed Sunita and informed her that Sunita did not know swimming.

When the teacher, Mrs. Laddha was apprised about this incident and that Sunita felt feverish, she did not take it seriously and gave her a paracetamol. Late that evening, Sunita's roommate informed the teacher that Sunita had developed high fever, that she was tossing and turning and mumbling something which was incoherent. Mrs. Laddha panicked. As the matter took a turn for the worse, Sunita was rushed to a government hospital. On the way, Sunita was still. Mrs. Laddha thought she had calmed down. The hospital declared her dead on arrival. The teachers were in a state of shock and decided to bring back all the children to Mumbai. Two teachers stayed back with Sunita's body and informed her parents. Students were told that she was in the hospital. Mrs. Laddha who was a friend of Sunita's parents convinced them that the teachers did their best and that it was destined.

Sunita's father came to terms with it and instituted the Sunita Memorial Award where he tried to remember the best of Sunita through the lived experience of kind and smart girl children. However, her mother went insane. Months after Sunita's death, her mother would put a blanket on Sunita's bed saying that she would catch a cold. A rumour that Sunita was sick beforehand started circulating unnecessarily. Some said that she must have had a heart problem. Others said that it was unusual that she never fell ill like normal children do. Mrs. Laddha felt that Sunita's mother should accept reality.

The gnawing feeling kept ripping through Sunita's mother that the teachers weren't probably close or inviting to Sunita and her problems. She wondered if she had expressed her problems to her teachers like she would to her mother. She contemplated if the teachers could have done better and been closer.

Will her questions ever be answered? Is the teacher guilty of negligence? Is there any point to this assignment of guilt? Was it destiny or a freak accident? Every teacher and student was mortally scared of a picnic or tour after this incident. Sunita's friends missed her terribly. One of the teachers of the school tried her level best to avoid any outing with students. The incident had left a scar in Sunita's family and hurt the psyche of the teacher.

Sometimes not expressing one's problem explicitly may result in serious consequences. Medical professionals believe that those who have higher ability to withstand discomfort or pain, may finally seek medical intervention when it is too late. As teachers and parents, we must find a way to be communicative and transparent of the problems or issues that our children face. And most importantly, be open and welcoming for children to say what is important and needed to us.

Heart

Sukanya got married into a traditional Bengali family living in Bhopal after her graduation in Mumbai. She had long hair and would drape her sari in a traditional manner. She always craved for appreciation from her mother-in-law which she seldom received. She tried to adjust in the joint family. Her husband, Subroto Banerjee, was loving and they had a lovely daughter, Isabelle.

Over the years, she also completed her Bachelor's in Education as a professional degree. Subsequently, she took up a job as a teacher in a missionary school. She was greatly influenced by the missionary brothers and Christianity as a lifestyle. The church's attitude, the father's disposition, the parish's helpful nature and the fights in the joint family drove both of them to convert their religion to Christianity. Their families did not want to do anything with them. The couple moved out with their child.

Sukanya got really busy with her household chores, school work and looking after the child's needs. Time really flew. She did not have time for herself and did not even object when her husband came home late. She got so completely engrossed in the day to day mundane work that she did not realize that she was putting on so much weight and was hardly presentable. Around this time, her husband started liking a girl in his office and their friendship grew. Some days, he did not even return home. Sukanya thought that her husband was working hard for the family. One has to work very hard in this competitive corporate world, she said to herself.

Soon after, Subroto started abusing her physically and mentally. He blamed her for the conversion and for separating him from his family. He would often come home drunk. One day when he came late and Sukanya questioned him, he started beating her. When Isabelle came to her rescue, he slapped Isabelle too and said that she was not his daughter. Isabelle was deeply hurt and realized that her mother was in this difficult situation because of her marriage and child birth. She only wanted her mother to be happy.

This was the last straw on the camel's back. Sukanya went to the missionaries to seek protection for herself and her daughter. Father Dominic understood the situation and transferred her from Bhopal to Ranchi, with accommodation close to the missionary school there. It was a relief and yet an uphill task for Sukanya to move there.

Her daughter, Isabelle, was extremely beautiful and kind hearted. She found it difficult to answer about her father whenever she was asked. Subroto had made a permanent scar in his daughter's heart. Isabelle had gone through a lot and found it difficult to deal with boys and men. Subroto had not only failed in the necessary duty of protecting his child but also instilled psychological trauma.

Sukanya didn't find inner peace. She was unable to see the troubles that lay in front of her eyes and couldn't act until it was too late. Can Isabelle ever be normal with men? Can she concentrate on her studies?

One cannot run away from one's roots. Individuals are free to assimilate knowledge from different sources and analyze. An escapist attitude shows that one cannot face reality and deal with it. There is no need for blind faith or loyalty. It is important to maintain mental balance and resolve.

Inequality

KUNAL HEGDE WAS the only child of his parents. He was born after twenty years of their marriage. He was loved and protected by his parents. They would bring him hot food during the lunch break. He would sit properly, use a napkin, and eat according to his mother's instructions. This continued even when he grew up. During his teen years, all the boys used to tease him. He would sit with the girls and have lunch. Slowly, he realized that he was different from other boys. He had no interest in football or cricket but loved dance. He was very fair and thin. He had artistic fingers and liked to paint his fingers and put on make-up. He even liked applying henna. After one of his dance programs in school, many commented that he looked prettier than the girls and danced better than them.

One day he was caught unawares in the washroom and the sports captain, Rakesh, abused him physically. Rakesh threatened Kunal with dire consequences if he reported the matter. After this incident, Kunal was reluctant to use the washroom. Kunal started absenting himself from school. He would give a lame excuse to his mother of being unwell. He was very respectful towards the teachers and in turn they were kind to him. However, he could not express his feelings and emotions and the problems that he was going through. He was courteous to girls who were kind to him but the boys shouted , "Chhakka" thereby implying that he was a transgender.

Humiliated beyond a point and unable to speak with his parents, he went more and more into a shell. He left dancing which he was so good at. His parents could not comprehend what happened to their son. Kunal was on the threshold of depression. These events had a deep impact as he became an adult and shaped his worldview. He became successful as a scientist but always had to hide his true feelings.

Why don't children feel comfortable talking about personal matters with their parents or teachers? Sexual orientation and gender are lived experiences of an individual, not a textbook or rulebook. The law has now changed too in the face of strident protests and moral arguments of truth and dignity. It is time we implemented it in letter and spirit.

Jealousy

Severe floods affected a southern state in India. School children in the northern part of India wanted to reach out. It was decided to hold a school fete before Diwali, the festival of lights. The Principal of the school did a brainstorming session with the teachers to allot stalls for the classes. A teacher of class eight wanted to have a stall selling earthen lamps known as diyas; others were keen to have food stalls and game stalls. Everything was voluntary. The students were motivated to buy from the stall since they were anyway going to spend on diyas. They were also encouraged to save the cracker money to light up the lives of the people in need.

One student, Shilpa, did not want to contribute even a single penny for the cause. She always had a problem with sharing. To make things worse, she was moody, disrespectful, and angry as well. On closer interactions, it came to light that she was very similar to her mother. Her mother was a control freak, penny wise and pound foolish. She was ready to pick up a fight for the smallest reason.

The girl who stood out like a sore thumb learnt her lesson the hard way! Although she did what she wanted and lived life according to her terms, Shilpa could not make herself happy. She was jealous of her cousin, Sumant who was an average student. Sumant was popular amongst teachers and students because of his amicable nature.

Looking at Shilpa's unhappiness, her mother felt guilty. She understood that it is the joys of sharing that make a person happy. She decided to mend her ways of her upbringing. She encouraged Shilpa to share her pocket money with poor children. She herself reduced her expenditure on luxuries and accompanied Shilpa to go to the blind school for donation. The more she was socially responsible, the happier she felt. She decided to volunteer at an old age home every week. One cannot pat one's own back, she realized. This transformation made them better individuals.

Coming back to the school fete, the diya stall did very well, contributing the second highest amongst stalls, first if considered section-wise. The students learnt organising and the art and science of management. People were generous and joyous. Students felt a sense of fulfilment and it was an experience of a lifetime.

Parents must inculcate a sense of social responsibility in children. As individuals, we should be kind to people in need and imbibe the same in our children. Sometimes, in spite of best efforts of the teachers it is difficult to bring in a change because of the family background. Strong roots of selfishness cannot be uprooted easily to make them humane.

Karma

Rose, ten years old and Velvet, five years old, were two sisters from a middle-class family. Their mother, Mary, was a nurse and father Jacob worked in an office. Due to a serious infection, Mary died in spite of the best treatment given by the hospital.

Jacob found it difficult to deal with the situation. His mother came to assist him, especially to manage the kids, but the winters would not suit her. She did not want to be a liability in the house. Jacob took up the responsibility of managing the home and the job. Rose would look after her younger sister Velvet and also assist her father in household chores. She herself was small but would wash the dishes, clothes and also clean the house.

Jacob met Anna at the workplace and started feeling affectionate towards her. Anna was divorced from her husband and had a seven-year old daughter Suzie. They decided to get married. Jacob thought that if he can be a good father to Suzie, Anna will be motivated to be an excellent mother for Rose and Velvet.

The initial months after the marriage were fine. It seemed to be a nice and happy family. However, in due course, Anna started showing her true colours. She took the entire salary from Jacob to run the house. With her salary, she pampered her daughter Suzie and saved for her future. Rose and Velvet were not allowed to sit and study. They were made to do all the household chores and Anna was very mean to them. She did not even give food to them properly. In front of Jacob, she would behave lovingly, else she would be very rude. She did not give any time to the children to speak to their father. Anna would monopolize all his attention.

The two girls were very adjusting. The teachers who knew about their plight would help them without making it obvious. Most teachers were loving to them and that is what they needed. Rose and Velvet grew into beautiful teenagers. They did well in academics. Suzie would find lame excuses for not getting marks. Anna blamed the teachers and took out her anger on Rose and Velvet.

Suzie could not develop a healthy relationship with anyone. She was a pampered and spoilt child who could not adjust in school. In college too, the problems only increased. She always blamed others for her mistakes. She spent a lot of money on clothes, fashion and make-up to be one-up on others. However, she was unhappy due to her own insecurities. Later in the work place too, the problems intensified. She was neither hardworking nor was she co-operative. She could not stick to one job and was also unemployed for several months before she got another one.

Anna was tired of life. She became hysterical at the slightest provocation. She would curse Jacob for everything. Anna did more harm to her own daughter Suzie than she did to Rose and Velvet. Jacob was scared of Anna and slowly stopped communicating with her.

Both his daughters loved him. As they were financially independent, they were willing to take care of him. He decided to stay with his daughters. Suzie, who was not used to working either at home or in a job, could not adjust with her old mother. Both of them could not find peace and happiness.

Excess of anything is bad, even love, gifts and money.

Let Your Hair Down

Sridevi was from the south of India. She was pretty and petite with expressive eyes, long wavy hair and wheatish complexion. She spoke English fluently with no grammatical error but was a little less confident in front of strangers. She was simplicity personified and was not comfortable with stylish people. During her school days, she was teased for her curly hair. She put water on her hair and combed it to show its actual length. Not only was she a good dancer, she was good in academics too. She got admission in a prestigious college.

Harsh, the basketball captain, teased her calling her "noodles". He had taken admission in sports quota and was not used to girls ignoring him. He had a great fan following as he won matches for the college. If Harsh teased someone, all the others would join him in chorus. Sridevi seemed to be indifferent to all these comments although it did hurt her feelings. Most of her friends suggested that she go for chemical treatment for straightening the hair which was not only expensive but might have also caused damage to the hair. She resisted.

A brilliant dance performance in the college auditorium for a formal function made her the star of the college and all the teasing came to an end. When she joined the private sector after her post-graduation, there was a feeling amongst people that corporate executives with curly hair looked unprofessional. She would always make a bun with her long wavy hair. Sometimes, she would absent herself on a bad hair day. Even when present, she would be under confident that impacted her performance.

Sridevi wondered about the mindset of people and who were they to determine what being "professional" is? It was when she became the CEO of a multi-national corporation that she let her hair down. She spoke her mind in an interview by a student leader in the campus where she was invited. "People weren't looking at my brains but focusing more on my hair. My complete focus was towards my work and doing things meticulously, trying to be better than the best. That is what mattered."

It is a fact that today most girls want straight and silky hair to gain appreciation. Some colour it blonde, some alter it permanently. No flower complains about its colour, texture or petals. They all have their specialty. Lotus is different from jasmine. The fragrance of jasmine is different from that of the rose. The swan is beautiful and so is the peacock. Deer is different from the tiger. Camel is unique as it is the only animal that can walk in the desert.

Whether you are fair or dark and you have curly hair or straight hair you are just fine. The various creams to make your skin fair and the chemicals that are used to make your hair straight may lead to cancer too, as per some surveys!

Teachers and parents might be well informed to keep their children away from material and physical evils which make them feel bad! And more importantly, children should understand that form is temporary, class is permanent!

Medical Madness

SHEHNAZ PASSED HER class ten exam with flying colours. Both her parents were doctors and there were a number of medical professionals in their family. They wanted Shehnaz to take up the medical profession. In their social circle, it was taken for granted that Shehnaz would pursue medicine. Shehnaz hated biology. She dreaded the dissection required in the practical curriculum. The sight of blood made her feel nauseous the whole day. Her parents understood none of that. When she did not perform well in biology, her parents decided to put her in a coaching center. She hated to attend those coaching classes.

Shehnaz went to the coaching center with the driver, Naved. Shehnaz was tall, fair with lovely tresses. She was aware of her beauty especially when Naved would look at her often. Over time, Shehnaz and Naved had developed a bond of friendship as he drove her each day. Parents kept scolding her and Naved made her laugh. He appreciated her beauty and she loved it. After the first term exam came the report card. Her performance was excellent in all subjects except biology. Her parents gave her a dressing down, called her irresponsible and that she was not concentrating enough. They also said that their hard-earned money was going down the drain.

After this incident, she started bunking coaching classes. She would leave home at the same time but go elsewhere with Naved. One fine day, she eloped with him. When she did not return home that evening, her parents panicked. They called up the coaching center only to learn that she had not attended class that day. They also learnt that she had been quite irregular. With great difficulty, her parents traced her and brought her home. This incident left an indelible mark and her parents realized that it is important for Shehnaz to pursue what she liked and be happy.

Her brother, Aman, who was just ten years old, started getting severe headaches in school. Before every exam he would get those unbearable headaches; otherwise, he was fine. He made friends easily and loved sports. While in the field he had no problems, whether it was bright and sunny outside or it was raining. All the clinical tests were conducted; no evidence of anything abnormal was detected. That meant it was psychological. Aman was a pleasant child and was loving towards everyone and loved animals too. He was an extrovert and a happy child. After the final exams of class five, the parents learnt about his poor performance in mathematics and science. Though they were disappointed, his parents were cautious and did not explore further. They tried to understand and empathize. They were less judgmental and more accepting. This helped the child grow in his sphere of interest.

Soft skills make a person more humane. Creative people can bring solutions to the problems of the real world. We must encourage children to do what they want to do and not belittle them. Parents should give supportive environment and avoid comparisons. This will allow children to realize their potential.

Nepotism

RAUNAK WAS IN class one. He was a bright and helpful child. Mrs. Anand, his class teacher, found him very responsible and competent. His parents were also co-operative. Whether it was organizing the class almirah or bringing and keeping note-books, she would call him. He did every work assigned by the teacher with joy. She took full advantage of this.

There was a story telling competition organized for class one students. Two students from each section were to be selected after listening to every student of the class. Raunak had prepared very well for this competition. It was not conducted on the scheduled date. The teacher had shortlisted three of the staff children for the finals. This fact was discovered much later by Raunak's mother. When Raunak's mother complained that he was not even heard, the teacher gave him a chance to speak after all the shortlisted students spoke and the judges were finalizing the marks. This seemed very unfair. He spoke extremely well and there was a thunderous applause.

It is so difficult to change the school, so he continued in the same school. In class six, due to shuffling of students of different sections, he was left alone in the new class and all his friends were in another section. There was an Inter School GK competition and students were chosen randomly. No one came to his section to announce the same. When his friends came to know that Raunak did not get the information, they were upset. They were sure Raunak would be a great asset for the team. They begged him to come as part of the audience. His parents agreed to send him although he did pour out his sad feelings to his mother of not being selected. The school lost the quiz. Maximum prizes were won by him as audience prize answering all questions that were unanswered by all the teams. His friends said that if he were part of the team, the school would have lifted the trophy. One of the teachers, who empathized with Raunak, told his mother that all this was the doing of the staff member who was very influential.

At this point, Raunak's parents wanted to change his school for obvious reasons. It was around this time that Raunak was declared first in an All India Science Talent Scholarship Exam across India. He was admitted in one of the most reputed schools in Delhi and did extremely well. In class twelve, he was chosen as the Head Boy, although he was competing with the son of a prominent member of the Board of Governors in the school. Every cloud has a silver lining.

Nepotism can really take a toll on the mental wellbeing of a sensitive child. It does not help anyone in the long run. Such unfair practices should never be part of any educational institution or society at large.

Over-protective Parent

PREMA WAS A pampered child. At sixteen, she was breathtakingly beautiful. A million hearts would flutter if she just walked on the corridors. She would update her profile on Facebook and feel elated with the number of followers or likes to posts. Prema was also into sports and co- curricular activities and shone like a star, though her academic performance suffered as a result.

Prema's mother was overprotective. She would sometimes behave in an immature manner and would hardly respond like a parent. In spite of the teacher giving two months' time besides the summer vacations for completion of the project, Prema had not even commenced work on the project. When the teacher gave an ultimatum, Prema soon submitted a detailed project. On reviewing the project submission, the experienced teacher could immediately sense that this was not Prema's work. When the teacher enquired in private, Prema admitted that her mother did the project.

The next day was Parent Teacher meeting. When Prema's mother came, the teacher narrated a story. The story was that of a young boy who could not see the butterfly struggling inside the pupa. He wanted to help and took it out. The butterfly died immediately. The boy started weeping uncontrollably. With tears in his eyes, he brought his mother to show what had happened. He also said that his intention was to help the butterfly. His mother explained "the struggle inside the pupa had to be undertaken by the butterfly itself so that when it comes out it is capable of flying beautifully". Prema's mother smiled and promised to allow Prema to grow. Her responses became more mature. Prema herself became more responsible and started balancing her academics with co-curricular activities.

Today all of us are proud of her. Along with being a fashion model, she is pursuing her MBA. She is confident and ready to take on the challenges of the world.

Allow your child to aim high, fly high. Sky is the limit! Help them develop their wings instead of flying them to their next destination!

Prized Possession

"YOU ARE AMAZING!"

"Superb performance"

"Splendid work"

"You are awesome!"

"There should be more people selfless like you."

Every time Ganesh felt a little low, he would take out these notes scribbled on paper and given to him by his teacher. This would boost his morale and make him more determined than ever to continue doing good work.

On a rainy day, as he sat on the table contemplating how to bring out the best in himself, he took out these notes. These notes were his treasure which he had kept safely in his school geometry box. He recalled an incident that happened in school. He was in class five then. He did extremely well in academics, particularly mathematics. In one of the class tests, he scored less marks. He was quite upset but did not show it. His mathematics teacher, Manisha Ma'am, came to the class during recess. She saw that Ganesh was sitting all alone. When she enquired, Ganesh started weeping uncontrollably. He recalled that he lost his mother when he was in class one. His mother was very proud and would be joyous at his smallest achievement.

After his mother's demise, his sister, Lakshmi, who was eleven years older than him, tried to fill the vacuum. Not only was she appreciative, she would look after him in every way. She would pack his lunch lovingly and take him to task if he did not study regularly. She would insist that he practice a number of questions and be thorough with the subject. She would sit with him late night if required till he was confident that he had prepared well for the exam.

Ganesh told his teacher that his sister had been married off recently and moved to Mumbai. As a result, he stopped bringing lunch to school and only money to eat from the school canteen. His father, Kanhaiyalal, a businessman, woke up late and returned home late in the evening. Ganesh did not have much interactions with his father.

Manisha Ma'am decided to help Ganesh. From that day onwards, they always had lunch together. She also told him to be more responsible and was firm with him. She taught him time management and also motivated him. She also helped him with school work on a regular basis. He won the first prize in an inter-school mathematics competition in which she had coached him. Both of them developed a special bond. She had become his second mother.

He did very well in academics, joined a reputed institute of technology and now works for a software company in the United States of America.

He never forgets to wish her on her birthday, Teacher's day and Mother's day. He always visits her when he comes to India and hosted her while she visited USA. She feels very proud of him and believes that no amount of money can buy this enduring bond.

Conscientious teachers make a positive impact on the students and influence their heart and mind, not only in school but throughout their life.

Que Sera Sera

Lalita was a dark-complexioned girl studying in class six. In most schools, when students are cast in a play as angels, it is usual to choose fair, rosy cheeked girls with long hair. When Lalita expressed her desire to be cast as an angel, her friends laughed! She complained to the teacher that she was an object of ridicule as her friends said that she can be cast as a witch. Lalita went home and wept.

Next morning, she did not want to go to school. Her mother was somewhat helpless but counselled her and sent her to school as she wanted her to face the world. Lalita, from that day, put on a mask. She became very reserved and did not interact much with anyone. She was polite with everyone but her heart was broken. She was average in studies and became an introvert.

She was feeling bad when some of her fair friends would eat an orange ice-cream and would show off their orange lips. One even commented that there is no effect of an orange ice-cream on Lalita implying that she was dark. She was upset when fair-skinned girls would show off their henna designs and comment that henna can hardly be seen in Lalita's hands. Lalita kept wondering if it was her fault. She absented herself on Children's

Day. She could not enjoy with her friends who would be dressed in casuals and look ravishing. She felt that there was no colour that suited her.

In class eleven, when she was selected for a dance on environment by an enthusiastic teacher , she could not believe her ears. However, she was apprehensive as she said that she did not know how to dance. "It is my job to teach. I only want co-operation and love to dance which I can see in your eyes", said the teacher.

The dance program on environment was a supreme success. She danced blissfully like no one was watching. Her mother had tears in her eyes. She blessed the teacher from the bottom of her heart. She had really gotten her daughter back.

Fair is beautiful is a concept deep in the minds of many, especially in India. The amount of sadness just due to complexion and the loss of confidence and self-esteem amongst students is such a disgrace on society. It is unfortunate that corporates are allowed to promote fairness creams and film stars are roped in to endorse such products. Imagine the irreparable loss that can occur to our future generations! Lalita was saved by the teacher and now holds a government job. We must give more attention to values and behaviour, brain and heart rather than physical appearance, skin and figure.

Rumour

"I AM A happier woman" said Muskan and threw a grand party when she adopted her son Shishir. Animesh and Muskan were married for many years. Animesh loved Muskan a lot but there seemed to be something missing in their lives. This is when Muskan decided to go for adoption much to her husband's joy.

When Shishir was old enough to join kindergarden, Muskan took his admission in the same school where she was teaching English. Muskan found Shishir's spellings apalling. He had no idea of phonetics and could not comprehend much. He was also distracted. "Is he dyslexic?" Muskan thought to herself as Shishir hugged her lovingly. In middle school, he was caught cheating red-handed. Muskan was very disappointed because she had not put any pressure. When Shishir was questioned, he said that all the students teased him for poor performance and so he cheated. He promised his mother not to do this again. He also said , heart of hearts, he knew that what he did was wrong.

One day as they were coming to school, the car had a punctured tire. Shishir said it was the happiest day of his life as he had a valid reason for not taking the mathematics unit test. He really hated mathematics. During the first term examination in class ten, Shishir had study leave. Muskan left for school in the morning as usual and Shishir was dancing to some Bollywood music. Animesh was doing his daily chores and he told Shishir a couple of times to sit and study. When Shishir did not listen, Animesh reprimanded him. As soon as Animesh left for office, Shishir went to meet his friends. He told them that he hated studies as also his father. "I want to escape all this", he said.

He decided not to go back home and eloped with his friend, Chhaya. On her return from school, Muskan found the door locked. She called up Animesh to find out if there was any information about Shishir as he was not at home. Animesh said that he expected Shishir to study at home. Muskan ran from pillar to post looking for Shishir. She called up her friends and relatives. She appeared to be calm from the outside but her mind was turbulent. She could not stop herself from thinking about his real parents. Animesh and Muskan were embarrassed. Finally, he was traced and brought back. That year Shishir failed in class ten. Parents were afraid to scold him after this incident. Right from food habits to manner and style of dressing, he would not listen to his mother Muskan.

Being one of the best teachers of value education, Muskan found it difficult to instil these values in her son. She also dreaded the day when he would ask them about his real mother. Shishir became a rebel. It was at this juncture that Animesh developed a heart problem. Muskan blamed Shishir's horoscope for bringing bad luck to the family.

The once-loving parents fell prey to superstition and negativity as a series of unfortunate events hit their happy family life. Animesh questioned the role of nature and nurture in the development of an individual. Muskan decided to put him in a boarding school as she felt they could not manage him. The family was now split and alone again.

Parents often feel that when their efforts don't yield results, it was somehow either a fault of their child or theirs. Sometimes it is neither. Each and every problem can't be fixed, whether real or imaginary. Having faith in the child is paramount to their success. Running away from a problem is not its solution.

Supergirl

Lalwanis were overjoyed. Chitra was born and there was a lot of happiness. Their family was complete as they already had a son.

Soon, they realized that Chitra was not normal. The doctor confirmed that the child was both physically and mentally challenged. Each and every person who visited their house, treated her like a museum piece. There was more curiosity than acceptance, sympathy more than empathy. If they took her to the temple, devotees would look at her rather than the temple idol. At the mall, some would ridicule her. They had to grapple with this situation. Mr. Lalwani found it very difficult to come to terms with it. Mrs. Lalwani decided to do whatever best can be done for Chitra. She put her daughter in Tamanna, a renowned school for children with special needs.

Mrs. Lalwani and the school together worked hard with Chitra. Chitra bloomed into a young teenager with excellent values, good manners and etiquette. She was very loving and everyone loved her. Chitra got married to Chirag Ratwani when she was 21. She was considerate to her in-laws and they were kind to her. A year later, Chitra and Chirag were blessed with a baby boy.

A couple of years later, Mrs. Lalwani opened a beauty salon for her daughter. She came every day to supervise and attend to the needs. However, after a while she made Chitra independent and started coming only once a week.

It is now a pleasure to see this joyful young lady who is financially independent and a role model for all of us. Her son is pursuing a graduate degree. She is extremely fond of him and one can see pride in her eyes when she talks about him.

Positivity and child-centered learning can lead to wonderful results.

Tit for Tat

SUNAINA LIVED IN Delhi with her father. Her mother was working in Dubai and would visit them once in two years. As a young girl, Sunaina missed her mother dearly. She needed her friend, guide and support system close to her, not in Dubai. She became anxious, stressed out and scared. Many a time, she wished that her mother would quit the job and return home. While her mother would promise to do that each year, she was not inclined to do so as she had a good lifestyle there, sans responsibilities. In fact, even during the holidays when she visited India, she would be looking forward to getting back to Dubai. The stress and strain of living here was overwhelming for her.

In due course, Sunaina came to terms with the situation. Now, in her teens, Sunaina found her mother to be glamorous during her visits. Sunaina started focusing a lot on how she looked and started wearing make-up like her mother.

Sunaina had become gregarious and had a large friends circle. She would always be conscious of her looks, hair and her physicality in general. She hardly spoke with her father.

A few years later, in one of the family visits to India, Sunaina's mother went for an annual health check-up. She was diagnosed with breast cancer. She had to undergo mastectomy and her family supported her in a big way. She was in no position to return to Dubai to continue her employment. During her many years of service, she had bought a house and a car in her native place. They all decided to live there. She took up a job in India but felt underpaid as she was used to overseas salaries and comforts. She went back again to Dubai after a few months much to the disappointment of her family.

After a year, when she returned to India, she went for another health checkup. This time she was diagnosed with cervical cancer. Again, her husband and their family took extremely good care of her and she fully recovered. She appreciated the value of family and found it irreplaceable. She vowed never to go back again. A few months passed, she noticed that her husband's appetite was slowly reducing. When she asked him, he said that it was fine and it was good that he was losing weight. However, after a few months, when he could hardly eat, they consulted a doctor. It was diagnosed as stomach cancer. This was shocking news and unbearable for her. Her devout husband soon left for his heavenly abode. Sunaina's mother kept ranting to all and sundry that her husband brought her back to life but she could not save him. It was her biggest failure.

Sunaina could not bear the loss of her father and decided to work in Dubai. Sunaina's mother realized how Sunaina would have felt then. Death is tragic because we cannot blame anything other than destiny for it. We blame the people around us for it. That puts the burden of tragedy on their life. This creates rifts filled with loneliness.

In the quest to earn material comforts and provide for the family, families are crumbling. Children feel lost if they are away even from one of their parents. What kind of a decision is this? At what cost? To have a child but not nurture it?

Universe

Seema was only a year old when her mother deserted her. She was brought up by her father, aunt, and grandmother. As she grew up, she saw kids hugging their mothers as they dropped them to school. Whenever a child was in difficulty, she saw them calling for their mother. Seema missed this kind of warmth. She would always search for her mother.

Whenever Seema asked about her mother, people would say a lot of nasty things. She found it hard to believe. There was always a lingering question in her mind if her mother had deserted her. Seema wanted to meet one person in the entire universe and that was her mother. She wanted to hear the story from her mother's perspective.

When she was in middle school, she returned home after school each day with a friend, her neighbour. One day, her friend was absent and she had to walk back alone. It was then that a lady in a burqa caught hold of her and hugged her. She removed the burqa and in a choked voice muttered that she was her mother. She told her that her father had warned her not to meet Seema and if he came to know he would harm the child. She added that they were unhappy with the dowry. They would harass her even when she was carrying Seema. When Seema was born, they were upset that it was not a boy. One day on a trivial issue, they just threw her out of the house.

"I am now working as a maid, washing dishes and cleaning homes as I am neither educated not financially sound. You are very precious to me and you must promise to study well, so that I don't have to see you suffering like me. I will not meet you again. Don't worry and he happy. My blessings are always with you.", said her mother as she hugged her and walked away.

Seema was in a state of shock when she heard all this. She did not say anything at home. From that day on, she focused on her studies and stopped asking questions about her mother. She remembered her mother's advice as to how important it was to become financially independent. Today, as she stands tall on her feet with a job, material comforts and the company of her real mother, she says that this is the best message that one can give to every girl.

Be real, be honest. Teach them to face reality.

Victorious Vijayanthi

VIJAYANTHI WAS A lovely child. She was tall, cute, good in academics, music and dance. At sixteen, she had a child-like innocence which reflected in her beautiful eyes. She was very sensitive and would cry like a little baby if students called her "moti" meaning fat girl. Every single day during her teen years, her weight bothered her. She forgot about her good height, translucent skin, lovely hair and pretty eyes. Everyone body shamed her.

She believed firmly that she was not attractive. She was short tempered and that made life tough for her. At the class farewell party, when she wore a lovely saree, some boys got vicarious pleasure and made mean comments. It upset her and she wept uncontrollably. She was counselled by her class teacher who made her feel positive about herself. It was not an easy task to calm her and make her feel confident, which required several interventions over the years.

Vijayanthi took part in various college festivals and her flair for English language made her stand out. She would be the anchor in many events and her compering was appreciated. She felt attractive now as she gained confidence.

Today she is the mother of a child and is managing her career wonderfully. Vijayanthi can never forget the calming and supportive hand of her class teacher.

Each one of us, as an individual, has a record button in our brain; the same incident affects individuals differently and every person keeps a separate memory of that incident. Shaming or bullying can seem like fun for some students but it can become a tragedy for the ones who are being picked on.

Most children who are fat feel that they are unattractive. They lose their self-esteem. Sometimes, they spoil their health by not eating a balanced meal, going for diet fads or diet pills. Short term weight loss leads to long term health problems. Healthy habits lead to positive change.

We The People

School is the place where values are formed. Untouchability, secularism and ahimsa (non-violence) are all values to be imbibed in school not only through day to day interactions but also through programs and thematic dances. In a dance program, roles are assigned according to the capability of the child. Each role is very important and is a significant part of the whole. The central character can be portrayed usually only by a talented student. However, each character is important for the whole to be complete.

It was the inauguration of the new school building held prior to the festival of Janmashtami. It was decided to organize a cultural program. One of the items was a dance drama on Lord Krishna, which was crisply done. Lord Krishna was played by a Christian girl, the garland that adorned her was made by a Muslim girl, Sana, and the mother Yashoda was played by a Hindu. Kalia Nag, the serpent, was played by a Sikh. People from all religions were part of the people under the mountain saved by Krishna or as Krishna's friends when the ball falls into the ocean. It was prepared well and presented to perfection.

The main role of Krishna was done convincingly by Margaret. However, after her mother faced some problems in the church, she declined to play roles of Ram, Sita and Kali in future programs.

She did not want her mother to feel bad or be ostracized from society. If classroom teaching of values conflict with societal values, it becomes very difficult for children. They get confused.

Sana was questioned by her mother who learnt that Sana had drawn a picture of Lord Ganesh for the classroom bulletin board and had made the garland too. Sana pleaded that she did it as an artform and not as religious practice. What is the harm in respecting all religions she thought. When students see that what we teach in school does not match their society or immediate family life, the void between theory and practice propagates hatred.

We all study the Indian constitution in the political science class in middle school. Is it to remain in the books only? We need to be very careful in our decision-making. When we question children and take decisions, we are planting seeds in their minds. If we plant a seed of hatred, and the society cultivates it, it will only lead to negative outcomes.

The seeds of hatred have to be removed like stage one cancer cells before they allow themselves to develop into something much more malicious. We must abide by the Indian Constitution that calls for respect to the individual liberties and collective freedoms that all of us must enjoy. Humanism, kindness and love are the most important religions.

X–Rayed

ZOHRA LOST HER father when she was just a year old. Her mother was married off again by her parents. Zohra's step father was supportive of Zohra's mother but did not earn any income. Zohra's mother would leave the child in his care and go for work. She would cook before she went for work and also after she returned from work. She was completely exhausted. Zohra's stepfather, Abraham, showed a lot of affection towards Zohra. He would kiss her and keep her on his lap. This made Zohra uncomfortable as she entered her teens. She felt somewhat suffocated from her step father's x-ray eyes.

One day when she returned from school, he abused her physically. He threatened Zohra with dire consequences if she reported the incident to her mother or anyone else. This became a regular feature. Zohra's mother and her maternal grandparents always trusted her step-father. They never saw through his mask. Now Zohra dreaded going back home after school. She preferred to hang out with her friends and sometimes would bring them home. Her step-father hated this. He would tell her that she cannot bring her friend home. Meanwhile, her mother developed kidney and heart complications and Zohra had to 'adjust' with her life. She decided that as soon as she starts earning, she would move out with her mother. Of course, she found it very difficult to concentrate on her studies but tried her best.

When such indelible marks are left in the minds of children there is bound to be a permanent scar and it is difficult for them to trust anyone at any time. However, the teacher could win her confidence and Zohra shared her problems. It was then that the teacher realized that in such a seemingly perfect family, there was complete chaos beneath the surface. The teacher kept this information confidential at Zohra's request and tried to help her in every way possible.

Today Zohra is financially independent and leading her life in a confident manner.

Express concern. Extend help. Timely counselling makes a world of a difference!

Yukta's Choice

YUKTA'S FATHER WAS employed in a public sector undertaking. He was transferred from Mumbai to Ramagundam. She, therefore, joined a new school in class ten. Not only was she good looking , she was very different from others. Tall and beautiful, she had a star quality. She had an artistic temperament and was very good in calligraphy. Her economics teacher advised her to take humanities stream in class eleven.

After the declaration of the class ten exam results in which she scored fairly well, she was confused as to which stream, such as science and commerce, she should take. Her friends had all taken science. When she spoke to her father, he said that if she is unsure it is better to take science, because one can always branch out later in college. Finally, she also chose the science stream.

Class eleven proved to be extremely tough for her. She could not cope up with physics and mathematics. Her father put her in coaching classes for all subjects. Yukta's self-esteem began to fall. She was also perennially tired. Somehow, with great difficulty she was promoted to class twelve. In class twelve, she became lonely. She had no friends. Everyone was discussing academics all the time. The once effervescent girl was always gloomy. Her parents were also helpless as she hardly communicated with them. They felt that she was just distracted and scolded her. They could not accept the fact that their daughter was incapable of pursuing science. They told her to concentrate on studies and restricted her outdoor activities as well as watching movies or playing mobile games.

Yukta went more and more into her shell, was highly anxious and went into depression. As expected, she could not clear the board exams and when the results came out, their entire family was shattered. They called her the black sheep. The school was also unhappy because they did not get 100% pass percentage.

A couple of years later, after being treated for depression, she completed her class twelve through the open university. She also did a course on textile designing and is a successful fashion designer.

We often fail to correct our small mistakes till it becomes unmanageable. Both parents and teachers should help the students and encourage them to do things in which they have a natural aptitude.

Zipping Up Feelings

Sunetra was a beautiful child. She topped her class every year. During her adolescence, she suddenly started fearing boys. This was in spite of the fact that she had two brothers. Sunetra would wear layers of clothing while dressing up as she was very conscious of how she looked. Even her gait had changed. She would walk with her head down, slowly but steadily. She was scared to even step out of her house as an incident had left a deep impression on her.

Once, when she was returning from school, a boy unknown to her touched her inappropriately and said that he wanted to be friends with her. She told him that she did not want to be friends with him and ran back home. After this incident, she avoided stepping out of the house, because she was scared that the boy may appear. Fear was so all consuming. After a few months, she agreed to go by bus. In the bus, a boy stood very near her where she was seated, pressing her and falling on her. She felt disgusted; she was not sure whether others in the bus would support her if she raised an alarm.

Sunetra kept quiet at home. She felt that there was no point narrating the incident but refused to go to school. Even within her house, she could hear boys laughing and she would close the doors all the time. She could also not sleep well. She would get a nightmare of such incidents which would wake her up sweating profusely.

Sexual harassment is taken so lightly in India. Girls are supposed to be strong and ignore all unnecessary overtures. We have to make them physically and mentally strong to repel such individuals and report such acts to the authorities. Not everyone can cope up. Sunetra was a survivor who couldn't find support and the consequences have been heartbreaking.

Mental illness among children is not recognized or diagnosed, leave alone treated. Many are not accepted if a child is fearful and schizophrenic. Kept hidden from the world, it marinates till it takes the form of a monster and no one can hide it anymore. Sometimes, we don't know what triggers one to take certain actions. Sadly, Sunetra is now in a mental hospital after these incidents went untamed and put her on an uncontrollable emotional spiral.

Sunetra definitely did not deserve this. It is the failure of parents, teacher and society at large if such things happen. Speak out! Support what is right!

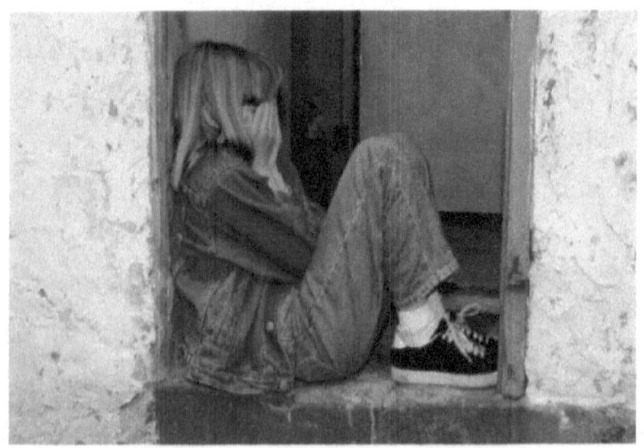

Happy Family, Happy Children

RAISING HAPPY CHILDREN is not as difficult as it may seem. The solution lies in accepting day-to-day situations and also exposing children to reality so that they become adaptable. Once this is accomplished, all anxiety will disappear.

- Angela was the eldest of three children. Her mother worked as a nurse in a hospital. She had to do night shifts on many days. Angela was capable of looking after her younger brother and sister happily even when she was very young. She was observant and knew that it was important for her mother to go for work. Communication between all the family members helped them overcome distress and difficulties.

- Padma was affected by polio as a child. She belonged to an educated middle-class family. She coped up with her difficulty and not only excelled in academics but also gave a dance performance. This could happen only because of her inner strength, a balanced upbringing by her parents and the school environment.

- Roshni, who was blind, was educated by her parents and now works for the blind school teaching English as well as arts and crafts. As she moves about cheerfully, no one can make out that she is blind. She has a lot of gratitude to her parents.

- Sapna is a doctor today, a COVID warrior. She comes from a middle-class family with two younger siblings. She learnt to cope up with the ups and downs of life when she was very young. Credit goes to her family for her upbringing. She is also a delightful mother.

RENEWAL

With the birth of a child, parents are reborn.

Grandparents live the childhood of their children.

There is revival of hope.

Monotony is broken.

There is much to rejoice.

Rejuvenation of everyone around takes place.

Child is the father of man and only a child can
tame the parents.

Conclusion

Parenting is an on-going process. Once a parent, always a parent. There is no escaping that and there is no mantra for right parenting. Most young parents feel that their duty will be over once the child completes school only to realize that the problems faced by college students are no less. Students need a lot of support so that they don't go astray. Parents then feel that once their son or daughter takes up a job and ties the knot, they can relax. Not for long. The young adults are stressed and need a lot of emotional support as they manage their home and career. The journey never ends. Sometimes, it is peaceful and joyous and at other times it is a tumultuous roller coaster ride. The bottom line is there are no perfect parents and no problem children.

Parenting in today's times is even more challenging due to easy access to information- too much, too early. It is like balancing and walking on a tight rope. There is only a thin line of difference between,

- loving and pampering
- guiding and controlling

- motivating and demanding
- supporting and spoiling
- making them self-reliant and making them isolated or dependent

The need to be tactful cannot be overemphasized. We also have to be careful with our tone. Sometimes, we take children for granted and they don't like it. Relationships sour as a result. That is the greatest tragedy, especially because deep down you care and a connection is cut off.

All the more reason to **handle with care.**

Similarly, teachers have difficulty in dealing with children. Once I heard a teacher commenting that super achievers cannot adjust with society and are difficult to handle. Such statements are tragic and we must retire them from usage. The Indian education system also forces teachers to follow procedures and instructions instead of creating an innovative environment centred around children. There is nothing admirable in creating repetitive and replicable robots. Falling in line shouldn't be rejoiced but rather questioned and mourned. Empower children instead of denouncing them! It is these children who can truly change the course of a nation and make a difference to the world.

I hope that this book is of help to young parents, to-be parents and teachers.

To conclude, I suggest we keep **LISTEN** as our mantra of success for parents and teachers in the following manner:

L	<ul><li>Love unconditionally</li><li>Live happily</li></ul>
I	<ul><li>Impress upon Integrity</li><li>Imbibe independent thinking</li></ul>
S	<ul><li>Simplify</li><li>Stress on values</li></ul>
T	<ul><li>True to oneself</li><li>Treat with respect</li></ul>
E	<ul><li>Encourage ethical behaviour</li><li>Emotional balance</li></ul>
N	<ul><li>Never neglect oneself</li><li>Nullify negativity</li></ul>

Down Memory Lane

THE SCHOOL OCCUPIES a very special place in the hearts of everyone. A whole batch of students return to the school to relive their time spent in the class, occupying their class and seats. They take out time from their work, travel from afar, leaving their family obligations behind to chitchat with their classmates. The child in them comes alive when they start performing role plays of the principal, various teachers, and even want to say the prayer together, like the good old times. Some bring their families and want their child to get admission in the same school. They introduce their spouses, show off their school, converse with the teachers and even meet the Principal. Their eyes glitter as teachers recall their naughty deeds and their achievements.

The life in school is indeed cherished by most.

Life comes a full circle when the story teller becomes a character in someone else's story. When I was writing this book, I asked some of my students to write about their experiences in school and the life that they lived beyond it. They touch various years and decades of my teaching career and somewhat different aspects or issues. However, the common theme is that I am proud to be their teacher and happy that I could contribute to their lives in some way.

Happy reading!

Manju Gupta

My school life was the best time for me. It was the time when I could meet my friends, have fun with them, free of tension and stress. I really enjoyed it a lot. But as I grew up, I had to face many problems. I belonged to a family where girls were not given freedom. Many boundaries were drawn. I had also lost my father and had many responsibilities. I did household work and helped my mother in business. When I was in higher secondary, I had to request for giving me some time to study, but I was allowed to study only after finishing all the work. So, I studied at night. Sometimes, I had to be awake whole night or even wake up at 3.00 am to study! I had to face electricity problems, as I lived in a village and power shut down was frequent. Then, I used candle or lanterns to study. In spite of all these obstacles, I never lost interest in my studies.

An important factor behind this was my teachers. They always supported me. Sometimes, I cried and shared my problems with my teachers and they used to encourage me (especially, Ramaa Shankar ma'am). I had a goal, that I will become independent, and I had to achieve that.

When I was just twenty-two, I cleared the entrance of DSSSB, and became a teacher in a government school. It was like, I got wings. I was happy with my job. However, infrastructure was always a problem. Students sat on the floor. In fact, they came to school, just because of mid-day meals. In the beginning, I had to teach the students in tents where no blackboard was provided. I had to carry a mobile blackboard with me. I still remember that I had to teach students under a tree when it rained heavily and tents were filled with water.

The absenteeism was very high in these schools. Parents were ignorant and were not able to understand the importance of education. I did my best to influence them to send their kids to school regularly. The COVID-19 pandemic has now forced educational institutions to conduct online classes. It is difficult for students too as most of the students belong to poor families and they don't have smart phones to use online applications.

We can only hope for the best in future. One day, we will overcome this situation and schools will again be the happiest place for students as they were before.

Chandra Thapa

I count myself amongst the fortunate ones to have passed out from a visionary school. Our school was amongst the best as its foundation was based on morals, integrity and values.

Our school is a symbol of knowledge because of the best teachers we have, always inspiring, Holding the ladder of success firmly for students, crafting us with patience, love and emotions and for me personally they are the real heroes. What we have accomplished today is all because of the hard work of our teacher.

It is rightly said by Aristotle, Those who know, do and those that understand, teach.

I was always a curious child during school with interest in sports and aviation. I was fortunate to be a part of the student council and also appointed as the sports captain of the school. After my schooling and college, I pursued my career in the aviation industry.

I am now with the best airlines in the world, Emirates, a global airline based in UAE. I have received lots of awards including the NAZM-The star award from our President, which meant a lot to me and the perk of flying free is an absolute delight. I am back to sports now and play cricket occasionally with my team mates. I am also a part of the sports culture in Emirates.

All I did was just to follow my dreams. At times, I fell short of steps but never backed out as every small step means progress towards the achievement of my DREAM. I always remember my favorite teacher saying, "BE PROACTIVE AND NOT REACTIVE".

I have always tried to live with this beautiful and realistic quote, which has always helped me to take some strong and correct decisions in my personal and corporate life. Thank you, Ramaa Ma'am for giving me this opportunity to share my experiences.

Archita Agarwal

We are all aware of the decisions we make in life, how it will impact our future and how it will shape us as a person. I have always cherished my school life. It was the best time I had in my life. The friendships and bonds that I created were genuine and will last a lifetime! I really enjoyed participating in Inter School competitions under the guidance of Ramaa Shankar Ma'am or working as a Head Girl. The school has always given warmth and love to all its students so now, wherever they go, a small part of our school stays with them.

While I studied a lot during class twelve, I scored lower than my expectations and had to settle for an evening college which was nearer home! In my first year, I really studied hard, topped my college which helped me get admission to a good day college in South Campus, New Delhi.

I strongly believe in "Love what you do and Do what you love". I did not find my dream job immediately. I allowed life to take its own course. I reached out to people whom I looked up to in case I got stuck. After completing my MBA, I got selected in a multi-national company and was in a high-pressure job for over nine years. During this period, I got married, had my daughter and it was a challenge to balance my responsibilities at home and office. I received great support from my family.

In 2018, something changed within me. I wanted to work for myself. I quit my job and ventured into entrepreneurship. I now spend substantial time in growing my online venture "Desi Sass" (www.desisass.com) which I started. We take pride in working directly with artisans all over India with the aim to blend our textile heritage with modern aesthetics.

Priya Nagar

Memories are like story books. They record our experiences and the lessons we have learnt from them. It is when we have quiet moments, or moments of introspection and reflection, that we allow memories to catch up with us.

Though I am in one of the top colleges in India, I could never really get my old school vibes over there. As far as I remember, the break time, physical education periods were seriously the time where we could really enjoy and spend some time with our favourite people; talking about each and everything, but I really miss every part of school. Even now, sometimes I see you all in my dreams, talking to all of you, maybe because I miss all of you a lot.

And my most favourite person, that's Ramaa ma'am. I don't think that anyone can ever replace you in my life... you are the second lady whom I love and care the most after my mother. I think you could have been a very successful astrologer. Seriously, hands down ... because I remember the things that you have said to me and somewhere deep down, I always knew that you were speaking the truth which no one ever could notice. I remember all the good as well as bad times spent with you and the lessons you've taught us.

I know that your style of teaching is very different as compared with others. Its uniqueness is the key to our gaining knowledge.

Kavita Awana

Whenever anyone asks me, "What was the best moment in your life?", there is only one answer. The golden days spent in school.

It has been fifteen years now. I still remember those days when we queued up for morning prayers, sharing the lunch, sipping from each other's water bottles, asking for extra pen, copying the homework, discussing most important questions before exams, missing friends in vacations, dressing up for the farewell and a final teary good bye hug to friends we grew up with. School memories are just so hard to forget, each and every moment was special.

Our school life has taught us a lot of things. The thrill of victory, the agony of defeat. There are moments in life that stay on forever. For me, it was the time spent during the last two years at school, especially with our beloved guiding light- Ramaa Shankar Ma'am. She taught us to have faith in our ideas, to be gentle with gentle people and tough enough to fight the world. I remember , I would try to hide my true self, but she was the only one who noticed me, trusted me and encouraged me at every step." You are her favourite student!" I have heard this phrase over and over in my plus two, I never denied it. I usually just smiled and nodded, yet everyone would still tease me. And I proudly say ...Yes! "I was Ramaa Ma'am's favourite student."

It's a pleasure to recall how you have shaped my life. As a teacher you taught various subjects but as a friend you told us to bravely face every storm. Whenever I feel low, I just remember your favourite song "Dil Hai Chhota Sa....Chhoti si Asha...." which you sang for us.

With tears of happiness and at the same time sadness, I remember how you would give me a bear hug and a gentle pat. You are truly an inspiration; mere words could never express my gratitude to you.

As I write this post, it makes me realize all the times we laughed, we cried, we won, we cared and we departed. My heart is filled with the best memories I could ever make. I would like to thank Rama Ma'am in helping me make such memories that would last for my lifetime.

School is never just a name. It will always be an emotion forever...

Parul Jindal

It was a privilege to have Mrs. Ramaa Shankar as my class teacher. She was a happy and charming lady. She taught us business studies and accountancy in classes eleven and twelve. She was gentle, kind and soft-spoken with a cheerful disposition. She encouraged us and explained the lesson to make it very easy. At times, she would be strict, if there was any indiscipline. I still remember the classical dance items taught by her and how she ensured that the postures were perfect.

I was deeply touched when she took the effort to bless me on my wedding day.

I cherish memories of my school and thank my parents for their decision to put me in this school. I fondly recall the morning prayers to everyday reading of a chapter in front of the class, the five-minute-masti to the graduation ceremony.

The values taught by my class teacher are fresh in my mind and as a mother of two children, I am instilling these in them and reliving my school life through them.

Alby Varghese

It is with great pride that I am sharing my thoughts and feelings for Ramaa Shankar ma'am; or how we profoundly called her Ramaa ma'am. With 'maa' or the word 'mother' being in her name itself says it all. She was a comforting mother to all her students and a breath of fresh air. A teacher who always looked out for her students' overall development and not just making them score well in the subject.

Higher secondary school was always very difficult but having such a responsible, passionate and enthusiastic teacher was a blessing. She always extended her positive energy towards all of her students and would encourage them to present their strengths and speak in the kindest manner to those who were struggling. She would reach out in a respectful and kind manner to her students, instead of focusing on what went wrong or what was missed. Ramaa Ma'am would encourage them to look ahead.

Ma'am would never fail to make lessons engaging and useful for all her students. She takes great efforts to go through each student's growth and gives appropriate and constructive feedback for them to improve. Her passion for dance had a contagious energy as well. I remember participating in multiple events in school only because she encouraged me to. Even when I would shy away from being on stage, she would always call me out and give me the push of confidence.

I now work as an accountant in Melbourne. When I look back, it is clear that my learnings from my teacher were the stepping stones for building my confidence. Till date, I have continued with the same spirit that she imbibed within me.

Arif Hussain

When I opted for commerce in class eleven, I was a lot anxious because I knew that I will be going into Ramaa Ma'am's class. Whoever knows me, knows that I was a bit off track in my class ten and that was the major reason for my anxiety for entering class eleven.

However, it turned completely different for me. I found the best teacher I ever had in my fourteen years of schooling. I wouldn't say one of the best because it would do injustice to the great human being Ramaa Ma'am is. She is undoubtedly the best teacher and there is no comparison. She supported me and my group of friends in almost everything, be it our studies, or guiding through our lives or the endless troubles that we found ourselves in. There were instances when we thought that we won't be getting the support of our class teacher but she proved us wrong. She was the main reason for me and my friends to change for the better in classes eleven and twelve. Even after leaving school, we remember her and we all know that whenever we need her, she will be there for us.

Writing this, still makes me feel nostalgic about my school days.

Trupti Roy

Principal's Day was announced. Ramaa ma'am was asked to present a dance item in a school program representing senior secondary students. She came up with a piece on women's empowerment, beginning from the epics, Ramayana and Mahabharata, and ending with the modern-day women.

When ma'am told me that she wanted me to play Draupadi and that it will be through spoken words, honestly, I was not sure if I would be able to do it. I was apprehensive whether I will be able to meet her expectations. But she was super confident. She sat with me and explained what she wanted out of the character. The best part about teaming up with her was that she trusted us and understood our potential better than we did. Although we had very little time to prepare, she would never allow us to compromise on our studies. Eventually our hard work paid off. The round of applause that we received did not only belong to our performance on stage but also to our mentor who worked for it and stood backstage.

That she was no ordinary girl
Was obvious with the little swirl
Born after two boys and much prayers
An allrounder and a natural dancer
Chanting "Lalitha Sahasranamam" right through the pregnancy,
Her mom was full of gratitude.
Known for her academic consistency,
Her father was proud of her attitude
That young lass was shining so bright, without a doubt,

A scholar, a daughter, a mother and a wife, she has come a long way
And shows perfection in every role she plays
But this journey wasn't to end soon,
Being righteous in her roller coaster ride, she is indeed a boon
It is time she shares her experience with all
Go tell everyone that dreams do come true
But only if you don't give up at all!